MAKING SOUNDS

Alan Trussell-Cullen

Australia • Brazil • Japan • Korea • Mexico • Singapore • Spain • United Kingdom • United States

Making Sounds

Fast Forward
Blue Level 10

Text: Alan Trussell-Cullen
Illustrations: Melissa Webb
Editor: Johanna Rohan
Design: James Lowe
Series design: James Lowe
Production controller: Hanako Smith
Photo research: Michelle Cottrill
Audio recordings: Juliet Hill, Picture Start
Spoken by: Matthew King and Abbe Holmes
Reprint: Siew Han Ong

Acknowledgements
The author and publisher would like to acknowledge permission to reproduce material from the following sources: Photographs by Getty Images/ John Stanton, back cover, p 14/ Taxi, p 15 top; Istockphoto.com, pp 3, 15 bottom; Lindsay Edwards, front cover, pp 1, 4-9, 11-13; Photodisc, p 10 bottom; Photos.com, p 10 top

ISBN 978 0 17 012542 0
ISBN 978 0 17 012537 6 (set)

Cengage Learning Australia
Level 7, 80 Dorcas Street
South Melbourne, Victoria Australia 3205
Phone: 1300 790 853

Cengage Learning New Zealand
Unit 4B Rosedale Office Park
331 Rosedale Road, Albany, North Shore NZ 0632
Phone: 0508 635 766

For learning solutions, visit cengage.com.au

Printed in Australia by Ligare Pty Ltd
5 6 7 8 9 10 11 20 19 18 17 16

THE UNIVERSITY OF MELBOURNE

Evaluated in independent research by staff from the Department of Language, Literacy and Arts Education at the University of Melbourne.

MAKING SOUNDS

Alan Trussell-Cullen

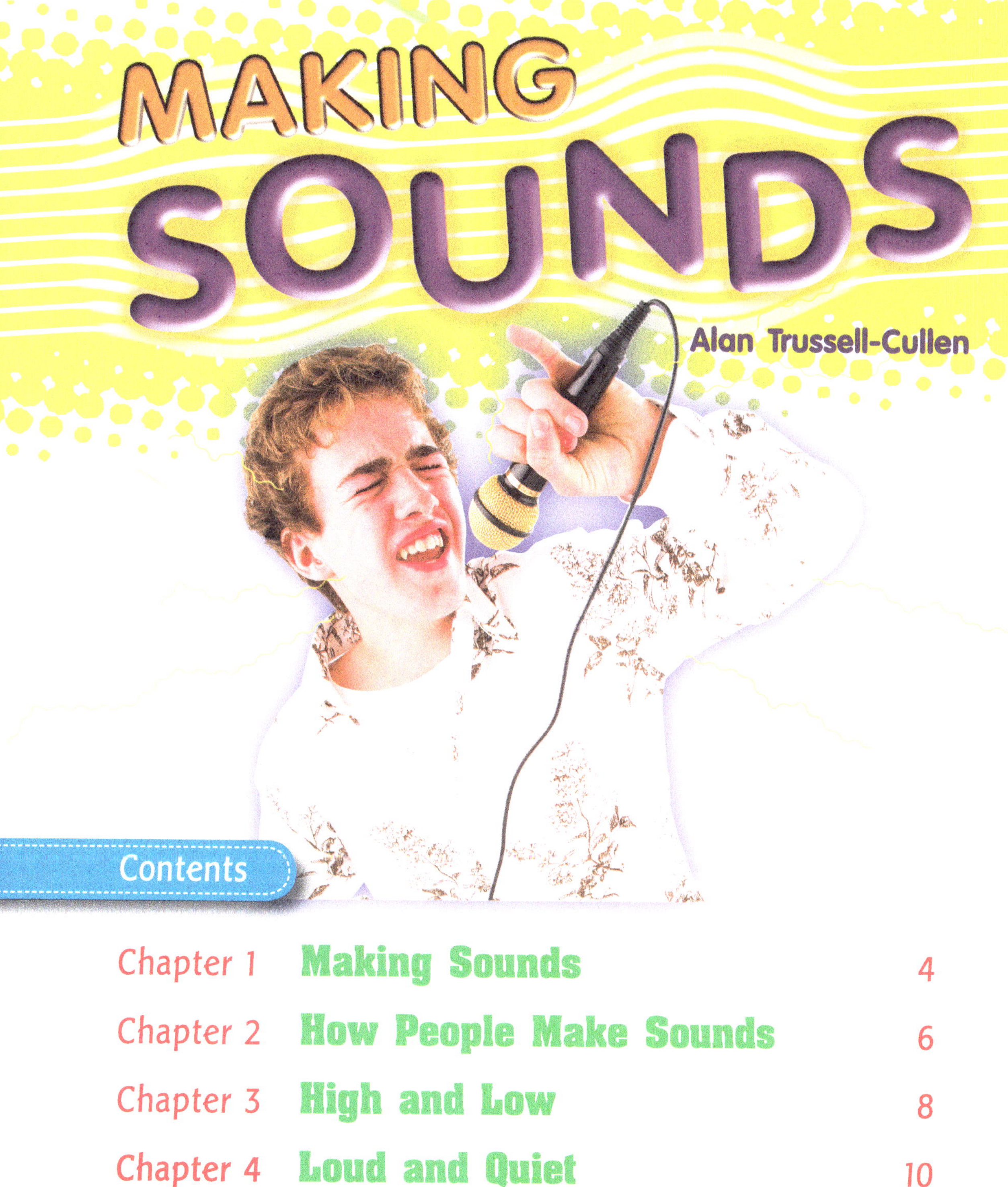

Contents

Chapter 1

MAKING SOUNDS

Sound is a kind of **energy** that is made when something **vibrates**.

Tap an empty can.
The can vibrates
and makes a sound.

Pluck a rubber band.
The rubber band vibrates
and makes a sound.

Blow air over the top of a bottle.
This makes the air in the bottle vibrate
and makes a sound.

HOW PEOPLE MAKE SOUNDS

People make sounds with their **voice boxes**. Sound is made when air comes out of the **lungs** and goes into the voice box.

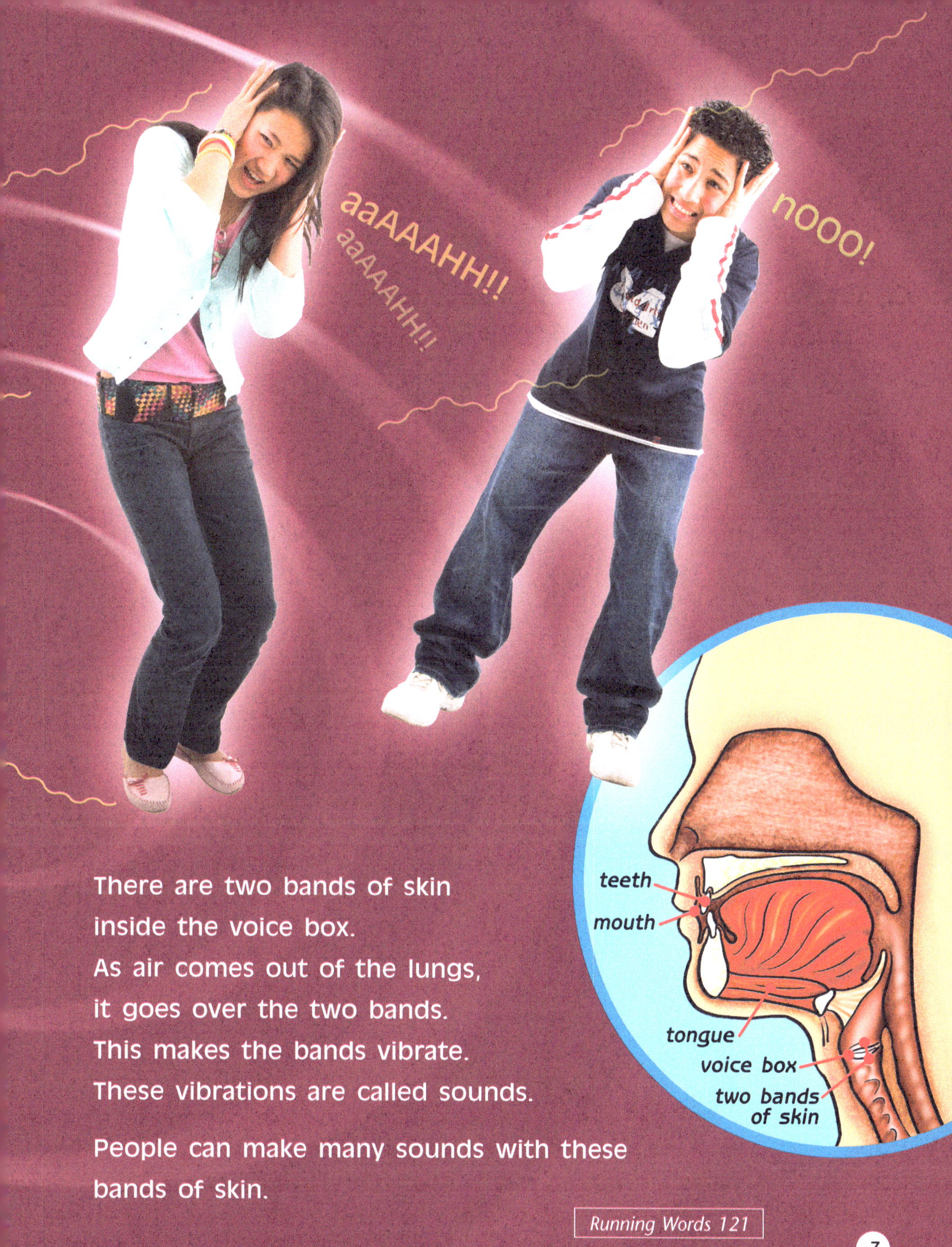

There are two bands of skin
inside the voice box.
As air comes out of the lungs,
it goes over the two bands.
This makes the bands vibrate.
These vibrations are called sounds.

People can make many sounds with these bands of skin.

Running Words 121

HIGH AND LOW

The voice box can make high sounds and low sounds.

Low sounds are made by slow vibrations. It's easy to feel the throat vibrating when the voice makes a low sound.

High sounds are made by fast vibrations. It's hard to feel the throat vibrating when the voice makes a high sound.

Chapter 4

LOUD AND QUIET

Sounds can be loud or quiet.

Fireworks make a loud sound.

This mouse makes a quiet sound.

Sound is an energy that travels around.
Loud sounds have a lot of energy.
They can travel a long way.
Quiet sounds don't have
a lot of energy
and can't travel as far.

Chapter 5

MEASURING SOUND

Sound is measured in **decibels**. Decibels measure how loud or how quiet a sound is. People can hear sounds from 0.1 decibels to 120 decibels.

A whisper is about 20 decibels.
A shout is about 114 decibels.

A band playing music can be as loud as 120 decibels.
The sound of a motorbike is about 120 decibels.
The sound of a plane taking off is about 140 decibels.

120 decibels

Sounds that are too loud
are bad for people's hearing.
Sounds that are louder than 120 decibels
can hurt people's hearing.

Hearing loud sounds for a long time
isn't good for anyone.

Glossary

decibels a unit of measurement used to measure sound

energy a power made by something

lungs organs within a person or animal's ribcage that allow them to breathe

vibrates when something moves rapidly to and fro

voice box an organ inside the throat that allows sounds to be made

Index